Delilah
and the
Dogspell

Also by Jenny Nimmo

Deilah and the Dishwasher Dogs
Deilah Alone
Hot Dog, Cool Cat
Seth and the Strangers
Ill Will, Well Nell
Tatty Apple

✧

For older readers
Milo's Wolves
The Rinaldi Ring
Ultramarine
Griffin's Castle

✧

The Snow Spider trilogy
The Snow Spider
Emlyn's Moon
The Chestnut Soldier

Jenny Nimmo

Delilah
and the
Dogspell

Illustrated by
Emma Chichester Clark

mammoth

For Ben, Josh and Tom

First published in Great Britain 1991
by Methuen Children's Books Ltd
Reissued 2001 by Mammoth
an imprint of Egmont Children's Books Limited
a division of Egmont Holding Limited
239 Kensington High Street, London, W8 6SA

Text copyright © 1991 Jenny Nimmo
Illustrations copyright © 1991 Emma Chichester Clark
Cover illustration copyright © 2001 Chris Priestley

The moral rights of the author, illustrator and cover illustrator have been asserted

ISBN 0 7497 4558 4

10 9 8 7 6 5 4 3

A CIP catalogue record for this title is available from the British Library

Printed and bound in Great Britain
by Cox & Wyman Ltd, Reading, Berkshire

Contents

1

Queen of the Night-garden

It is after midnight; Delilah knows that this is a special time when humans sleep and cats are queen. It is her first night in a new home. She misses Almira, her mother, and she misses Mustapha Marzavan, Breeder-of-Rare-Cats, her master and protector. Above all, she misses Mustapha Marzavan's youngest daughter, whose gentle hand and soft voice taught her that humans can be as kind and comforting as mother cats. 'Don't be afraid of leaving us, Delilah,' Mustapha Marzavan had said. 'You will always be safe, because I have given you the gift of magic.'

Delilah surveys the night-garden with wide golden eyes and the dark world gives up its secrets. Even the tiniest mouse, holding its breath in a far corner, is not safe from her. But Delilah is not concerned with mice just now, she can smell something fierce and eager. It is still a long way off but every heartbeat brings it closer. It is a dog and it is seeking her out. From the roof of her skull to the tip of her tail, Delilah freezes.

The dog is large and has a huge voice that crashes in on Delilah's thoughts; for a moment she is confused and this makes her even more afraid. The creature is right below her now. It throws itself against the wall, trying to reach her, its horrible roaring voice paralyses her. She needs her mother's wisdom; she needs Mustapha Marzavan's strength, but they are far away. Delilah must protect herself.

Delilah is angry. Her anger spirals through her grey coat in bright threads. Her glow illumines a dog's big muzzle and dirty yellow teeth. He looks amazed. Delilah is sparkling like the coloured candles in Mustapha Marzavan's great cat-parlour. She is crackling like an electrical storm. She wants the dog to be as tiny as a kitten, as miserable as a half-eaten mouse; she wants his voice to be as soft as Mustapha Marzavan's youngest daughter's. Delilah utters her wishes aloud and they take flight in a brilliant cloud of stars that cascade from her whiskers; they settle on the dog like tiny embers, burning his coat, his tail and his muzzle.

The dog begins to dwindle. He grows smaller and smaller and smaller. His voice fades and his coat falls apart; it floats away in big hairy patches.

Now it is the dog who is afraid. He cries out in a tiny voice, his naked tail droops and he races away as fast as his short legs will carry him.

Delilah stares after the dog without an ounce of pity. After all, he would have done worse to her. She settles herself on the wall, proud and secure, queen of the night-garden. She will never be afraid again. She knows she is a witch!

2

Annie Meets Delilah

Annie Watkin was swinging on the front gate. She liked doing this better than anything else because, while she was swinging, she could watch what was going on in the street. Annie always felt lonely in the school holidays. All her friends lived on the other side of town; the children in her street were teenagers and too old to play with Annie. She had often asked her parents for a baby brother or sister, even a kitten, but they didn't seem able to manage any of these things.

'Maybe,' Annie's mother would say. She was a very tidy person; perhaps she didn't like the mess a kitten would bring.

'One day,' Annie's father would say. He was very fond of listening to operas on his music centre; perhaps he didn't like the noise a baby might bring.

Annie swung on, dreaming herself into a place where you could play with cats or cuddle babies all day long, and then something surprising and interesting happened. A huge removal van pulled up outside the house next door. The house had been empty for as long as Annie could remember; she had often wished a friend would come to live there, someone with a kind mother who would talk to Annie's mother over the garden wall. Was her wish about to come true?

The removal men had almost finished their work when a long white car drew up behind the van. Three people got out: a man in a dark suit, a very glamorous lady with her nose in

the air and someone small, just Annie's size. She began to feel excited and made the gate swing faster. Creak-squeak! Creak-squeak! The small person turned round. Annie's heart sank. It was a boy and he didn't look very friendly. The family began to walk up the path into the house, but the boy changed his mind and walked towards Annie. He was carrying a long wicker basket.

'Hello!' he said. 'I'm coming to live next door. What's your name?'

'Annie,' Annie replied.

'Annie, meet Delilah,' said the boy and he opened one end of the basket.

Annie found herself looking at the fiercest cat she had ever seen. It had eyes as yellow as dandelions and fur like wild smoke, all grey and curling. Its whiskers were long and silvery and it had an unusual turned-up nose. The strange cat was sitting on a red velvet cushion and wore a collar studded with sparkling crystals.

'Delilah's won prizes,' said the boy, 'for her beauty.'

'Oh!' said Annie, rather surprised.

Delilah gave her a strange misty look as though she knew exactly what Annie was thinking.

'I got her for my birthday. She's foreign and very rare.'

'I should think she is,' said Annie, who thought Delilah looked more like a fairy-tale creature than a comfortable everyday sort of cat. 'Could I . . .?' Annie began. 'I mean, do you play with her?'

'Never,' said the boy. 'She's too fierce. She never purrs.'

'Oh!' Annie was so disappointed. A cat living right next door and she couldn't even play with it. At least there was the boy. 'What's your name?' she asked.

'Edward,' he replied. 'Edward Pugh.' He was about to tell her more when his mother called from the door, 'Edward, what are you

doing? Come and unpack this minute.'

Edward sighed. 'Got to go now,' he said. 'Mum doesn't like me to hang about. I think I'll give Delilah an ice cream; we've been in the car for ages and she needs a treat as much as I do.' He closed the basket and walked away.

Annie wondered if he would like to come and play later on but she didn't know if he was the sort of boy who played hide-and-seek or tig. Before she could find the right words to ask what games he liked, Edward had disappeared into his new home.

I'll tell Mum, Annie thought, then she can make friends with Mrs Pugh and maybe I'll get to stroke that strange cat. I'm sure there's a purr in it somewhere, just waiting to come out.

She was about to run indoors when she heard a funny little sound coming from the other side of the wall. She opened the gate and looked out. Sitting close to the wall was a tiny dog. He was very thin and bedraggled; his fur was matted, his ears were bald and his tail had been bitten.

'Where did you come from?' asked Annie.

'I got stuck in that removal van,' said the tiny dog with a whimper.

Annie could hardly believe her ears. 'D-d-
did *you* speak?' she asked at last.

'I think I did,' said the dog. 'Yes, I'm sure I
did, I mean I am speaking, aren't I? I'm as
surprised as you are. I've never done it before.
It must be part of the dogspell,' and he gave a
long sad whine.

Annie had been told not to touch strange
dogs but no one had ever said anything about
a talking dog. He looked so sad and lonely,

like a little lost child; she just had to pick him up. She carried him into her garden but the dog began to cry as though his heart was breaking. His tears soaked Annie's jumper so she gently set him on the ground. 'Oh, please don't cry,' she said, 'I'll help you. What's your name?'

'Prince,' said the dog through his tears. 'Don't laugh. I *was* a prince yesterday. I was tall and broad with lovely thick fur. I had a beautiful home and a kind mistress called Dora Bell – she's famous, you know. And then I made one silly mistake.'

'What did you do?' asked Annie, all agog.

'I chased Delilah,' Prince told her.

'Do you mean the strange cat that's come to live next door?'

'That's the one,' said Prince. 'She used to live near us. She's a witch, you see. She's done terrible things to my friends.'

'What sort of things?' asked Annie, although she wasn't sure if she really wanted to know.

'She shrinks dogs,' Prince said in a low voice.

'No!' Annie was horrified. 'Does she do it to humans too?'

'I don't think so,' said Prince. 'As far as I

know, she only does dogspells. I knew it was dangerous to chase her but I've got my reputation to consider. She had just turned my best friend Hodgson into the tiniest dog you ever saw, and he used to be monumental. It was a horrible sight, she was crackling like a firework while poor Hodgson got smaller and smaller. Well, as I was renowned for my bravery, I couldn't let her get away with it, could I? So I leapt up to bite her tail, but before I could reach her, great sparks shot out of her whiskers and I felt all shivery. When my paws touched the ground again I was – like this. I was so ashamed and so horrified I ran and hid in that removal van. But I got locked in and now I've lost my home and my looks and . . . everything,' and the poor little dog gave one of the saddest howls Annie had ever heard.

Annie was quite shaken. Could a cat really turn a dog into a tiny creature with a human voice? And if she could, what else might she do?

3

'I think I'm shrinking!'

'What's that terrible noise?' Annie's mum shouted from an upstairs window.

'It's this poor dog,' said Annie. 'It's lost. Can I give it something to eat?'

'Are you sure it's a dog?' asked Mrs Watkin. 'It looks more like some kind of rodent.'

'It's a dog,' Annie insisted, 'and it's hungry. It'll die if we don't feed it.'

'Don't touch it, Annie,' warned Mrs Watkin. 'It might bite.'

'It doesn't bite, Mum,' said Annie. '*Please*! Can I feed it?'

'All right,' said Mrs Watkin, reluctantly. 'Get a bone out of the bin.'

'I'm sorry about Mum,' Annie apologised to the dog, 'but she's a bit funny about animals. Follow me.' She led Prince into the

kitchen where her dad was cooking himself a second breakfast.

Annie's dad was very tall; two metres and two centimetres to be precise, and he wore glasses. The ground was so far away from his face he didn't see it very well, so he often tripped over things. He worked at the concert hall; Annie wasn't sure what he did there, but when he was at home he was always humming and waving his arms about like a musical windmill.

'That's a nice little kitten,' said Mr Watkin when he saw Prince.

'It's a dog, actually,' Annie told him.

Mr Watkin took off his glasses and bent as low as he could. 'So it is,' he said. 'I thought you wanted a kitten, Annie.'

'I did,' said Annie, 'but this poor dog is lost. Can we look after him until his owner comes to fetch him?'

Mr Watkin scratched his chin. 'I think we ought to take him to the police station,' he said.

Prince howled mournfully, on and on and on. Tears poured down his furry cheeks and made a pool on the kitchen floor.

'Oh, please can we keep him until the police find his owner,' Annie begged. 'It would be really mean to lock him up. And I can play with him until you find a kitten for me.'

'He doesn't look too healthy,' her dad said doubtfully.

'What an awful noise,' cried Mrs Watkin running into the kitchen. 'Annie, take that dirty dog outside at once. Look at the mess it's made!' Mrs Watkin was much closer to the ground than her husband, she noticed every tiny speck of dust and every little drop of water.

'It's only tears, Mum,' said Annie.

'Tears, my foot!' exclaimed Mrs Watkin. 'OUT, dog!'

'Don't call him dog, Mum. His name is Prince,' Annie begged her.

'Titch would be more appropriate,' observed Mrs Watkin. 'Come on, out with him before he makes another puddle.'

Prince now howled louder than ever.

Annie picked him up and ran into the back garden. 'Don't cry,' she said soothingly, 'I'm sure everything will be all right. I'll look after you until we can find your mistress.'

'But she won't recognise me,' wailed Prince, 'even if I tell her who I am. She won't believe me. I was, well, just magnificent!'

'Hm!' said Annie, doubtfully. 'What you need, right now, is a good meal. Hunger is making you depressed.' She hunted in the dustbin and found the bone from last night's supper. Prince looked a bit offended but he gnawed at it quite happily until Edward Pugh peered over the wall.

'What a funny-looking animal,' Edward remarked.

'He's a dog,' Annie told him. 'He's lost and very hungry. I suppose you know that your cat . . .'

Before Annie could say another word, Delilah leapt on to the wall with a horrible hiss. She arched her back, swished her tail and glared at Prince who immediately dropped his bone and ran under Mr Watkin's car. And Annie couldn't blame him, Delilah looked capable of anything.

'What a soppy dog,' said Edward. 'He's scared of a little cat.'

Annie wished he hadn't said that. 'Well, he told me that your cat was a witch,' she said, trying not to look at Delilah.

'Don't be silly,' said Edward. 'Dogs don't talk and Delilah's not a witch.'

'She is,' Annie insisted. 'That dog had a lovely home and a kind mistress until Delilah shrunk him. I can't believe you didn't know what she was up to.'

Delilah made a deep, threatening sound in her throat, half a laugh and half a hiss. It made Annie's scalp tingle and Prince was so upset he started to cry again. His mournful whines brought Mr Watkin rushing out. Bending

under the car he said, 'You can stop that noise, dog. I've rung the police and the R.S.P.C.A. and they say it's all right for you to stay with us, for the time being.'

When Prince said, 'Thank you,' Mr Watkin jumped up so fast that he hit his head on the side mirror.

'Good grief!' he cried. 'Did I hear that dog talk? I'd better go and sit down. I can see stars.' He staggered indoors, falling over the back step as he did so.

'Your dad's a bit peculiar, isn't he?' Edward remarked.

'He's very kind and very musical,' Annie said huffily.

'My dad hasn't got time to talk to dogs,' scoffed Edward.

'Does he talk to you?' asked Annie.

'Not much,' Edward sadly admitted. 'He's far too busy. So's Mum. They bought Delilah to keep me company. Mum doesn't like other children in the house. She says they spoil her things.' He lifted Delilah rather gingerly off the wall. 'Delilah may be fierce, but she's my best friend,' he said. 'So don't you ever call her a witch again.'

Annie noticed that Edward held Delilah very carefully as if she were made of

porcelain, not flesh and fur. The strange cat twisted in his arms, stretched her front paws up to his shoulder and stared back at Annie with her fierce dandelion eyes. It made Annie shiver. She imagined a rabbit must feel like this, caught in the headlights of a car. She couldn't move until the boy and his cat had disappeared and then she called in a panicky voice, 'Prince, come out quickly. I think I'm shrinking!'

The little dog crawled out and glanced round anxiously. 'You look just the same to me,' he said.

'Are you sure?' cried Annie. 'I feel all peculiar.'

'I'm sure,' Prince replied. 'You're huge!'

'Huge?' shrieked Annie. 'You mean I'm growing?'

'No,' said Prince impatiently. 'You've always looked huge to me. Anyway Delilah only does dogspells. Her magic doesn't work on humans.'

'Oh, if you're sure . . .' Annie was so relieved she ran and hugged the little dog.

'It's so unfair,' grumbled Prince. 'I've never harmed anything in my life.'

'But you chased Delilah,' Annie pointed out. 'And so did all those other dogs. Can you imagine what that's like? Some dogs have terrible barks and great ugly teeth. Delilah must have felt so angry and so frightened. If I had a cat I would always keep it safe; I'd stroke it and play with it and I *know* it would purr.' Annie sighed. 'But Mum and Dad can't seem to find one for me.'

Prince wriggled out of her arms and walked away from her. Then he lay down and put a paw over his face, but Annie didn't notice.

She wasn't shrinking. She was happy and huge. Well, normal anyway.

'I almost feel sorry for Edward. His parents are too busy to talk to him and his only friend is a cat who doesn't purr.' At last she became aware that Prince was lying in a silent sorry huddle. 'What's the matter now?' she asked.

'It's easy to see where your sympathies lie,' Prince muttered unhappily. 'But would you mind, just for a moment, paying me a bit of attention. How would you like to be a tiny creature with hardly any fur? Winter's coming on and no one will have me indoors looking like this. I shall freeze to death.'

'Oh, forgive me,' cried Annie contritely. 'I'd forgotten how bad you must be feeling. There must be a way to make you into your real self again. We'll just have to think really hard.'

'I'm not used to thinking,' grunted Prince, 'but I'll have a go.'

So Annie and Prince sat on the swing and thought hard. This didn't work so they went into the front garden and thought and thought until it was time for Annie's lunch. In the afternoon they sat on the wall and thought, and then it began to rain.

'I can't stand this,' Prince complained. 'My

coat doesn't seem to be waterproof.'

'I'll smuggle you indoors,' said Annie bundling him under her sweater. 'But whatever happens, don't talk. It'll only upset my dad.'

Mr Watkin was in the kitchen trying to compose a tune on the milk jug. 'Your mum's just popped next door with some tea for the new neighbours,' he sang out. 'She's been looking forward to having a chat with them.'

Annie was about to sneak a biscuit under her sweater when her mum came in looking very upset. 'That Mrs Pugh isn't very friendly,' she said sadly. 'She didn't want my fruit cake and she prefers coffee in the afternoon. And she told me not to bother her again because she's very busy.'

'Poor Mum,' Annie sympathized. 'They're not going to be very good neighbours, are they?'

Before her mum could answer Prince gave a loud sneeze. Annie tried to put a hand over his nose but found the wrong end of him and pinched his tail instead. Prince leapt out of Annie's sweater with a yelp. Mrs Watkin dropped the tea-tray and Mr Watkin ran out of the kitchen saying he'd lost his tune.

'Annie, now look what you've done!' Mrs

Watkin complained. 'I told you to keep that dog outside.'

'But it's raining, Mum,' Annie objected. 'And his fur's coming out. He'll get a cold. He's sneezing already.'

'Dogs don't catch cold,' said Mrs Watkin. 'Put him in the tool shed!' Prince gazed up at her with a 'Please be kind to dumb animals' expression, so she added, 'You can give him Dad's old cardigan, seeing as he's hardly got a coat of his own.'

'Thanks, Mum,' said Annie. She wrapped Prince in her dad's woolly cardigan and carried him out to the tool shed. It was beginning to get dark and thunder crackled in the distance.

Prince seemed rather nervous about being left alone. 'Would you kiss me before you go?' he asked Annie shyly. 'I've heard that a beautiful girl can turn an ugly creature back into a prince, with a kiss.'

'Of course, if you think it'll help.' Annie bent down and planted a kiss between Prince's bald ears.

Nothing happened.

'Ah, well,' sighed Prince. 'It was worth a try!'

'I'm sorry,' said Annie. 'But I'm sure we'll

think of something tomorrow. Try and
forget your troubles and have a good sleep.
Sweet dreams!'

She closed the shed door softly and then
went to look over the wall at the Pughs'
house.

All the lights were on but they must have
been too busy to close the curtains. Annie
could see into every room. What fine

furniture they had. Big gold mirrors, silky sofas, beautiful paintings and thick coloured rugs. They must be very rich, Annie thought. But that didn't give them the right to be rude about her mum's cake.

The rain had stopped but the garden was still wet and glittery. The grass shone and the leaves sparkled in the light from the uncurtained windows. Everything looked mysterious and magical. There was even a pale shape, like a tiny ghost, moving under the trees.

Annie glanced up at the Pughs' house. No one was looking. She was a little afraid but she was also very curious and, before she had really thought about what she was doing, she had heaved herself on to the wall and dropped into the Pughs' garden. Very cautiously, she tiptoed after the strangely gleaming shape.

4

The Sky-dogs Are Growling!

From her high window Delilah watches the rain. She hates all things that are wet, except warm milk, of course!

The storm has made the world dark and, above the trees, the sky-dogs are growling.

Delilah doesn't want to be a queen tonight. She doesn't want to go into the cold drizzle where strange dogs with huge voices snarl behind the clouds. But someone is going to make her go out. Mrs Pugh lifts her up and carries her downstairs. Delilah struggles; she spits and hisses.

'Don't be silly, Delilah!' says Mrs Pugh. 'It's stopped raining. You know you've got to go out.'

'But the sky-dogs are growling,' Delilah protests. She repeats this over and over again, in her loudest voice, hoping that someone

will understand.

'What's that all about?' asks Mrs Pugh.

'I don't think she likes the thunder,' says Edward.

'Rubbish!'

Delilah wishes her magic worked on humans; only claws can be used in this situation, but if she scratches they will be cross with her, they might leave her outside all night. Delilah spits anyhow. Mrs Pugh dumps her on the back step and closes the door.

Delilah runs for the trees. Her paws slip on the muddy ground and the wet leaves drip on to her fur. Her anger grows; it sizzles through her whiskers and little sparks shoot into the darkness, spinning off the leaves like tiny stars. But Delilah's magic is useless here. It is beautiful but it doesn't make her warm, and it doesn't stop the sky-dogs from bullying in their thundery voices.

All at once Delilah sees something hanging in the trees. Has the moon dropped out of the sky? No, it's a face. The girl next door has been hiding in the garden, watching her.

They stare at each other, saying nothing. Delilah wonders what the girl is thinking. She can't be a friend for she is protecting Delilah's enemy, that stupid dog who tried to bite her tail. And yet – perhaps the girl could be a friend. She reminds Delilah of someone.

The girl is gazing at the starlit leaves, at the brilliant colours that Delilah's anger has thrown into the night. She seems to be admiring the magic, and yet she is afraid of it.

Delilah wants to tell the girl that her spells can't hurt her. She wants to say: 'I am just a cat, like any other, who likes warm milk, soft cushions and a bright fire. I like to be stroked and carried and comforted but, sometimes, when I am angry, things happen!' Delilah wants her voice to be welcoming but she has lost her purr; it was swallowed by the anger that grew inside her when dogs started chasing her. Delilah is afraid she may never find it.

'Annie, what are you doing out there?' calls an anxious voice from next door.

The girl backs out of the trees, slowly, still looking at Delilah.

'Good-night!' Delilah miaows politely.

But Annie just looks frightened and runs away.

5

Prince Has a Plan

Next morning Mr Watkin was in a very bad mood. 'Mr Pugh has parked his car right at the end of our drive,' he said. 'Now I can't get my car out and I want to fetch the Sunday papers before the shop shuts.'

'Tell him to move his car!' Mrs Watkin was almost as tetchy as her husband.

'I have,' Mr Watkin told her, 'but they've got two cars and there's only room for one outside their house. And Mr Pugh says he can't put his car in his garage yet because it's full of boxes.'

'You'll have to run to the shop, then,' sighed his wife. 'I do wish our new neighbours were friendly. All my life I've longed for someone to chat to over the garden wall.'

'Neighbours!' grumbled Mr Watkin as he

pulled on his trainers.

Annie wasn't really listening to her parents. She was thinking about last night. Delilah was such a wonderful and extraordinary cat. She wished Edward had seen the crack and sizzle of her whiskers and the fiery stars that leapt about the trees. It had all been very scary and yet, afterwards, Delilah had looked at Annie in such a thoughtful way, almost as though she had been trying to tell her something. 'I wonder . . .' murmured Annie.

Her mum gave her a funny look and said, 'It isn't the car that's worrying your dad, it's Dora Bell.'

'What?' Annie sat up. Dora Bell was Prince's mistress. 'What's happened to her?' she asked.

'No one knows,' said her mum. 'She was due to appear on a television charity show last night. But she never turned up. You know she's your dad's favourite opera singer. He was really depressed.'

The mystery was solved the very next minute when Mr Watkin bounced into the kitchen waving a newspaper. 'There's a picture of Dora Bell in the paper,' he cried. 'She didn't appear on television because she was too upset. Her dog has disappeared and

she says she'll never sing again if he's not found.'

Mrs Watkin took the paper and read aloud, '"There has recently been an unusually high percentage of dog disappearances. In fact it has just been confirmed that even Hodgson, the prime minister's dog, is missing. In the past few days the P.M. has become increasingly bad-tempered and forgetful, and it has been suggested that the disappearance of his favourite pet has caused this uncharacteristic behaviour."'

'I must see how Prince is getting on,' said Annie, slipping out of her chair.

The little dog was still asleep when she looked into the tool shed.

'Prince,' she said urgently, 'wake up!'

Prince reluctantly opened one eye and yawned. 'What is it?' he asked sleepily.

'Come out here,' said Annie. 'I've got to talk to you.'

Prince shook himself and walked, blinking, into the bright morning.

'Listen,' said Annie. 'Your mistress, Dora Bell, says she'll never sing again if she can't find the real you. And now the prime minister's dog has disappeared. It must have been Delilah!'

'It was,' Prince sadly agreed. 'Hodgson was my best friend. I can't bear to think about it.' Tears rolled down his nose and made a puddle on the path.

'Hello!' said a voice. 'Don't tell me that dog's crying.' Edward Pugh grinned over the wall.

'Yes, he is, and it's all because of your cat,' said Annie accusingly. She was glad that

Delilah wasn't with Edward. 'Why won't you believe me? She's put dogspells on hundreds of dogs, even the prime minister's, and he's so upset he's forgetting everything. You've got to do something about it, Edward! She's your cat.'

'You're all potty!' croaked Edward. 'I mean really potty,' and he couldn't stop laughing.

From somewhere inside his tiny frame Prince found a deep menacing growl. 'Stop giggling, you stupid boy.'

'Wh-wh-who was that?' Edward suddenly looked frightened.

'It was me!' roared Prince, leaping on to the wall.

'It's a trick,' stammered Edward. 'I don't believe in talking dogs.'

'You'd better believe it,' said Annie. 'Delilah bewitched him.'

'Rubbish.' Edward backed away from them. 'My Delilah's a good cat. She's won prizes. She doesn't make spells. That dog's just jealous because he's tiny and mangy and smelly!' He stuck out his tongue rather nervously and ran indoors.

'That boy has really nasty manners,' growled Prince. 'I think it's time I taught him and his family a lesson.'

'How can you do that?' asked Annie.

'I've just had a brilliant idea,' he told her. 'I don't know why I didn't think of it before. I'll have to get in touch with a few friends, of course,' he went on thoughtfully. 'And it will be more effective if we do it at night.'

'What are you going to do?' begged Annie, bursting with curiosity.

'Wait till tonight,' Prince winked a beady eye, 'and you'll see!'

That evening the little dog ate a hearty supper of Mr and Mrs Watkin's leftovers outside the kitchen door. They were so cross and so disappointed about their new neighbours they had barely touched their meal. Annie had managed a few mouthfuls but she had felt very uncomfortable with her parents looking so glum.

'I hope this plan of yours works,' she said when she kissed Prince good-night. 'My mum and dad are really miserable. You don't think you could get the Pughs to move away, do you?'

'Maybe,' Prince yawned, 'but I think it would be better to scare them a bit, make them feel they need a friend.'

'I suppose you're right,' said Annie. 'Come to think of it, I'm sure I could get on with Edward if he wasn't so pleased with himself.'

Annie gave Prince one last pat and tiptoed out of the shed, but just as she was about to close the door Prince called out, 'Don't shut it, please. I'll be going out later.'

'Oh, yes, I forgot,' Annie whispered. 'Good luck!'

She went to bed earlier than usual so that she could watch the shed from her bedroom window. She was so excited she thought she would never get to sleep, but the next thing she knew she was lying on her bed without any covers and a very strange noise was coming from somewhere.

Barking! That's what it was. And not only barking but howling and whining, snarling and snapping. There must be hundreds of dogs outside.

Annie jumped off the bed and ran out on to the landing. Her mum and dad were standing by the upstairs window.

'There must be something wrong with my eyes,' said Mr Watkin anxiously. 'I can see hundreds of tiny little creatures in next-door's garden.'

Annie peered out. There *were* hundreds of tiny creatures in the Pughs' garden. Dogs! All of them as small as Prince, and they were howling and yapping in rather high, mysterious voices.

'There's nothing wrong with your eyes, Harry,' said Mrs Watkin. 'I've never seen such funny-looking things. They're a bit like Annie's stray dog. I wonder what they're doing next door?'

Annie knew but she wasn't telling. Prince had brought his friends round. All the friends who'd had dogspells put on them. They were

tiny, weeny, scruffy, mangy little animals with wonderfully strange voices.

Annie raced downstairs. She wanted to be part of the fun.

Her mum shouted, 'Annie, where are you going? It's after midnight and you haven't got your slippers on.'

'I just want to have a closer look, Mum!' Annie called back and she ran outside, forgetting that the dangerous Delilah was still lurking somewhere.

The Pughs' garden was an amazing sight. It was jam-packed with dogs and there was Prince, right at the front, barking louder than any other dog. The Pughs had run out without putting on their dressing-gowns. Edward was banging a frying-pan, Mr Pugh was waving an umbrella and talking to a policeman, and Mrs Pugh was leaping at the dogs with a broom.

Annie jumped up and down with excitement. 'Good old Prince,' she sang. 'Edward will have to believe us now!' But all at once, she didn't feel so bouncy. A horrible tingle ran down her spine and she found herself looking up at a high dark window where two glowing eyes stared into the garden.

'Delilah!' Annie murmured. 'She's going to do something, and this time it'll be even worse than before. Run!' she cried to the dogs. 'Run away, quickly, or something terrible will happen to you. Delilah's going to cast a spell.'

None of the dogs heard Annie. They were making far too much noise. The window where Delilah sat suddenly blazed bright blue; green sparks crackled against the windowpane and pink stars whizzed round Delilah's head. Her wild fur fizzed with furious spells and her eyes burned like fiery gold.

The Pughs had their backs to the house but the dogs could see the witch-cat now. They were looking up; their howls died and their jaws dropped in horror. And then – they vanished!

'No!' cried Annie. 'Prince! Prince! Where have you gone?'

The policeman stared at the empty garden in amazement and walked back to his car, shaking his head.

Mr and Mrs Pugh seemed rather embarrassed to find themselves out of doors in their nightclothes but Edward had spied Annie and he gave her an anxious smile.

'You know what Delilah's done, don't

you?' cried Annie. 'She's made those poor dogs vanish. You must have seen it.'

Edward wandered over to her. 'You don't think they just ran away, do you?' he asked hopefully.

'Of course they didn't,' said Annie. 'Delilah – dissolved them!'

'She couldn't have,' Edward protested.

'Edward, come to bed,' called his mother. 'And you ought to be in bed, too,' she shouted at Annie. 'It's after midnight. Whatever are your parents thinking of?'

Annie didn't want to go to bed. How could she sleep when Prince and his friends had been turned into nothing. 'Oh, Edward, what are we going to do?' she said.

'Looks as though I'll have to try and think of something.' Edward wrapped his arms round himself to stop shivering.

At last, thought Annie, he does believe it's Delilah's fault.

'Edward! Bed! This minute!' screamed Mrs Pugh.

'I must go,' he said reluctantly and trailed back to his mother, 'but I'll see you in the morning.'

Annie began to hope that Delilah's dreadful sorcery had at least made Edward her friend.

6

Ghosts!

'Annie, you'll catch your death of cold standing on the wet grass in nothing but your nightclothes,' called Mrs Watkin.

Annie just stared at the empty space where, only a moment before, Prince and his friends had been howling so ghoulishly.

'Did you see it, Mum?' said Annie. 'Did you see how all those little dogs just vanished.'

'It did seem a bit strange,' Mrs Watkin admitted. 'But I expect they ran away, very fast. We're all so sleepy we're probably imagining things.'

'I didn't imagine it, Mum,' said Annie. 'Prince was with them and now he's disappeared too.'

'You need a good sleep, Annie,' said her mum. 'Your little dog will probably turn up in the morning.'

But the strange night wasn't over.

As soon as Mrs Watkin had kissed Annie good-night and closed her bedroom door, Annie became aware that there was something in her room. Something alive. She could hear its heavy breathing.

Annie was terrified. She thought Delilah might be hiding under her bed. Then it was as

if something very large had jumped up beside her and thrust a wet nose into her face. Annie screamed.

'Sssh!' said a familiar voice. 'It's only me.'

'Prince!' whispered Annie. 'Oh, Prince. Where are you?'

'I'm sitting on your pillow,' said Prince. 'You can't see me because Delilah has made me invisible. But I think that cat has overspelled herself this time. She forgot to take our voices and our bites away. We can play a few tricks!'

'What sort of tricks?' asked Annie.

She was answered by three terrible screams from next door.

'The ghostly sort,' Prince explained with a doggish chuckle.

Annie looked out of her window. The Pughs were in their garden again, still in their nightclothes, only this time they were standing as far away from their house as possible.

'Help! Ghosts!' cried Mrs Pugh. 'Help! Help!'

Mr Pugh and Edward were trying to get her back into the house but she wouldn't budge. And who could blame her? From inside her new home came long eerie howls and mournful whinings. If Annie hadn't known what they were she'd have been scared too.

At last the invisible dogs tired of the fun, their voices became hoarse and their howls died away. Only then did Mrs Pugh allow her husband to lead her, shivering, into the house. But before she left the garden Annie heard her say, fretfully, 'Those Watkin people should have warned us the place was haunted. Not very neighbourly, are they? I'm leaving here tomorrow. My nerves can't stand it.'

'Give it a chance, Mum,' said Edward. 'I'll get rid of the ghosts for you. I think I know how.'

'Don't be silly, Edward,' said his mother.

'That was a great trick,' Annie told Prince, 'but it's not going to make the Pughs any friendlier.'

'Edward is coming on nicely,' said Prince.

'Poor Edward.' Annie tucked one arm round an invisible furry neck. Prince seemed to have become much larger than he was when she could see him. 'Something to do with the spell, I suppose,' she murmured.

'What was that?' grunted Prince.

But Annie had fallen asleep.

She woke up to find her mum bending over

her. 'Annie, that boy next door wants to see you,' she said.

Annie jumped out of bed. 'It's very early,' she yawned, pulling on her socks. 'What does he want?'

'Don't ask me,' her mum sighed. 'But he says it's urgent. If only we had nice neighbours,' she muttered as she left the room.

Annie got dressed and went downstairs. She found Edward sitting in the hall and looking very glum.

'Well?' said Annie. 'Have you decided what to do about Delilah?'

'Not exactly.' Edward seemed to find it necessary to whisper. 'But I believe what you said about her. She's made all those dogs invisible, hasn't she? It's really creepy in our house. We keep bumping into furry things we can't see, and then there are barks in rooms where we think we're private, and there's nothing there. It's horrible. My mum and dad are in a terrible state. Dad keeps throwing the china about and Mum's locked herself in her bedroom. She keeps screaming about werewolves.'

'You'll just have to make Delilah remove all her dogspells,' Annie told him.

'I know,' Edward said, 'but she's run up a tree. She wouldn't even come down for a choc–ice. I think she's scared. Oh, please help. I'm sorry I was mean to you. I really wanted you to be my friend but I always seem to go about these things the wrong way. I haven't got any friends at all, only Delilah. I know she's wicked but she's so beautiful and I l–l–love her.' A tear trickled down Edward's cheek and Annie couldn't help feeling sorry for him.

'Cheer up, Edward,' she said. 'I'll help you to rescue Delilah but you must stop her from making any more spells.'

'I will if I can,' Edward promised. 'But if she's a witch it's going to be a bit of a problem. I mean, she might turn me into something.'

'She can't,' Annie told him firmly. 'Now go home and get a box, and I'll meet you in your garden.'

'OK,' said Edward doubtfully.

As soon as he had gone Annie ran up to her bedroom. 'Prince,' she called softly, 'can you come and help? Delilah's gone up a tree and she won't come down.'

There was a loud thump on the bed as Prince wagged his tail. 'Only too pleased,' he said. 'I'll go and get the lads.'

Annie felt something furry brush past her face. She heard heavy pawsteps on the stairs and followed. The pawsteps led her across the hall and into the kitchen.

Mr Watkin was standing by the sink with a cup of tea. 'Good morning, Annie,' he said. He took a step towards her and bumped into something, dropping his cup of tea. 'Help! I think I'm going blind,' he moaned. 'There's a horse in here. I felt it but I can't see see it. Oh,

dear! Oh, dear! Oh, dear!'

'You're just tired, Harry,' said Mrs Watkin.

Annie ran to open the back door. 'Out!' she said to Prince. 'Before you cause any more trouble.'

'Annie, there's no need to speak to your father like that,' said her mum.

'I was talking to the dog,' Annie told her impatiently.

Her parents gave her an anxious look as she ran out, so she closed the door firmly behind her. She didn't want them to worry about the things that were about to happen.

Prince was enjoying a furious barking session now. Very soon Annie heard hundreds of pattering paws. She felt the crush of hairy bodies pushing against her. Although they were invisible the dogs didn't seem to be small any more. Some of them touched Annie's shoulder. It was a very strange sensation, like standing in a stream that was all hard and furry.

'Hello!' Annie said to the invisible dogs. 'I'm so glad you could all come. You've been having some fun with Delilah by the sound of it.'

There was a chorus of doggish giggling and excited cries of 'You bet!' 'I pulled her whiskers!' 'I hid her cushion!' 'I bit her bottom!' 'She can't see us!' 'She's scared stiff!' 'She can't do a thing!'

'I hope you didn't hurt her,' Annie exclaimed. 'After all she's only a little cat.'

'A witch!' Prince reminded her. 'However, I have a plan. I shall climb the tree, very quietly, and give Delilah such a fright she'll jump out. My friends here will catch her, then you and Edward must put her in a box and keep her there until we decide what to do next.'

'I've told Edward to fetch a box,' Annie said, pleased with herself for thinking ahead. 'But, wait a minute. I didn't think dogs could climb trees!'

'Invisibility has great advantages,' Prince assured her. 'I'm lighter than a bird.'

Edward was standing, with his box, beside a tall spindly tree, and perched at the very top was a round smudgy shape with little sparks popping out of it, like a firework that hasn't quite finished exploding.

'There she is,' yelped Prince.

'Raaaaah!' the dogs howled eagerly, and Annie was almost carried along by the pack of invisible animals that swarmed over the garden wall. Then she was whirled towards Delilah's tree in a sea of furry bodies. Edward was nearly flattened against the tree-trunk.

'What's happening?' he cried.

'Don't worry, Edward,' Annie called out breathlessly. 'Prince has an idea.'

'This *is* a rescue operation, isn't it?' Edward inquired nervously.

'Everything's going to be all right,' Annie said confidently. Actually, she wasn't so sure. She was beginning to fear for Delilah.

'He's going up now,' a husky voice informed her. 'I'm Hodgson, the prime minister's dog. I'm Prince's best friend. He'll save the day. He's a great dog, Prince is.'

There was an expectant hush, then leaves rustled and suddenly the whole tree began to shake. An angry hissing sound came from the tree-top. Delilah was whirling round and round like a catherine wheel.

Snap! Snarl! Yelp!

Hiss! Spit! Shriek!

A battle was taking place. But who was winning?

They soon found out. All at once, and with an ear-splitting caterwaul, Delilah leapt out of the tree. She spun earthwards like a furry meteor and landed on the heaving backs of hundreds of invisible dogs.

'Yeeeee-ooooowl!' screamed Delilah as the dogs bounced her towards Edward. 'Ssssss!' she hissed as they tickled her with their invisible tongues and nudged her with their wet invisible noses.

Then a mysterious force, that must have been an unseen and very tall dog, picked her up by her crystal-studded collar and dropped her into the box.

'Sorry, Delilah!' said Edward as he slammed down the lid. 'Now what do we do?' he asked Annie.

Annie wasn't sure.

7

A Witch in a Box

Delilah glowers in the dark box, imprisoned! Her fury explodes and bounces back on her. She can't reach the dogs with her spells.

Something has gone wrong. She isn't a mature witch yet.

How dare Edward put her in a box? And as for the girl, Delilah had thought Annie would be kind to cats, she had such a pleasing cat-friendly voice. She reminded Delilah of someone who had been as close to her as her own mother. And yet, for some reason, Annie was encouraging those hateful dogs.

Delilah wants to be bad. Very bad. Her magic may not be strong enough but she can use her claws and her teeth. And yet, if she is too bad, she might lose a friend, and she needs a friend. She needs someone to help her find her purr!

8

The Dogs Make a Promise

The box began to jump about as Delilah raged inside it, scratching, biting and tearing at the cardboard.

'We're not going to let you out until you take off all your spells,' said Annie, tapping on the box. 'Please be reasonable, Delilah. It's for your own good.'

Delilah was quiet for a moment; perhaps she was thinking. Then she began a furious attack on the cardboard again.

'I'll never give you another choc-ice!' Edward shouted, holding down the lid with a shaky hand.

Delilah spat through a hole she had made and Edward nearly dropped the box. 'This isn't going to work,' he moaned. 'I can't keep the box shut much longer. What shall we do? Think of something, someone, quickly,

before Delilah explodes this thing. She is a witch, remember!'

'I don't think she can do that,' Annie said. 'Her magic only works on dogs.'

'She doesn't need magic,' cried Edward. 'She's as fierce as a tiger, and tigers eat people!'

Annie's mind raced. Was Delilah afraid of anything? What did she hate most of all? She remembered the cat in the wet garden, and her angry spells leaping round the trees. It gave Annie an idea, a very dangerous idea because Delilah might do anything. But it was a risk they'd have to take.

'She hates water,' Annie said.

'Brilliant!' yelped Hodgson. 'Let's give her a bath!'

'I don't think . . .' Edward began. But his voice was drowned by a hundred barks of 'Come on!' 'Give her a bath!' 'That'll do it!' 'Let her find out how it feels to be cold!' 'And wet!' 'And miserable!' 'And shrunken!'

Edward was pushed and shoved into his house and Annie found herself being carried along behind him on a wave of excited, yelping, invisible dogs. On the stairs they passed Mr Pugh who cried, 'Help! Ghosts again!' and jumped over the banisters.

Up and up they went, along the landing, past boxes and crates and Edward's mother in her petticoat, and then they were in the bathroom, which was very large and gleamed with shiny mirrors and brass fittings.

'Annie, turn on the taps,' Hodgson commanded.

Annie put the plug in the bath and turned on the taps.

'I'm sorry about this, Delilah,' Edward said to the box, 'I really am, but if you don't take the spell off all these dogs, they'll – er – drop you in the bath, so, please, for your own sake . . .'

Annie was impressed. She could see how hard it was for Edward to treat Delilah this way, he had screwed up his eyes to stop the tears and looked quite desperate.

'Meeeooow!' shrieked Delilah, and she began to leap about in the box, almost rocking Edward off his feet.

'Edward, open the box!' ordered Hodgson. 'It's time to show Delilah we mean business.'

As Edward dutifully opened the lid, Delilah's scowling face appeared; her long silver whiskers were sizzling with rage. She glared at Annie who still had one hand on the bath tap and Annie's heart thumped as a pair of wild yellow eyes beamed straight at her. She could see the witch-cat's shoulders hunching, ready to spring, and Annie was quite sure she would have been torn to shreds or shrunk to a crumb if something hadn't grabbed Delilah by the collar again and swung her over the bath. She looked very funny, hanging in the air, spitting sparks into the bathwater. The room echoed with howls of laughter – even Edward and Annie had to giggle.

'Take the dogspells off us right now!'
growled Hodgson through invisible clenched
teeth. 'I can't hold your collar much longer.'

Delilah wriggled and spat, she hissed and
screeched until the room boiled with her hot
steamy breath. Then, suddenly, her back feet
touched the water and she became deathly
still. A low grumbling mumble came from
her. The bathwater began to bubble, it turned
pink and purple and green. A soft twinkling
mist filled the room which went so quiet
Annie could hear the beating hearts of a
hundred invisible dogs, all waiting to become
themselves again.

Something was happening in the bathroom. Through Delilah's starry magical mist, a dog's head appeared, and then another and another. Delilah might be dreadful but Annie couldn't help feeling a tingle of admiration for her. Furry bodies were

appearing now; some big, some small and some medium-sized; white, black, brown and spotty. There were so many dogs they were standing on the basin, on cupboards, on shelves, on the lavatory and even on each other. And there, holding Delilah by her collar, Hodgson was now recognisable as a magnificent Alsatian.

'Oh, Hodgson, thank you!' cried Annie clapping her hands.

There was a roar of approval as Hodgson swung Delilah away from the bath and plonked her in the box. With a triumphant growl the big dog began to lead the others out of the bathroom, but Annie hadn't finished with them.

'Just a minute,' she said. 'Before you go I want you all to make a promise.'

The dogs stopped and looked back at Annie.

'You must promise never to chase cats again,' said Annie, 'and then there won't be any more trouble!'

There was a stunned silence. The dogs looked at Annie as though she was quite mad.

'I know it's in your natures, but I think it's only fair,' Annie went on firmly. 'After all, if we make Delilah promise not to make dogspells again, shouldn't you make a promise too?'

The dogs were appalled at Annie's suggestion but after a while could see that she was making sense. They barked out their promises, a little reluctantly, and then the joy of being themselves again overcame them. They bounded along the landing, down the stairs and out through the open door.

Annie and Edward could hear the lively

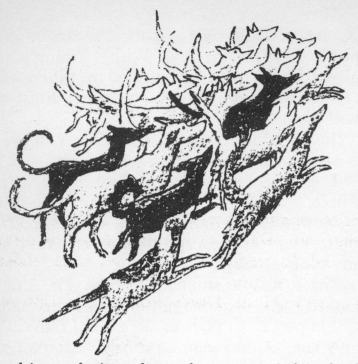

barking echoing along the street. A hundred dogs, free of dogspells, were going home again. All except one.

'Edward, where's Prince?' said Annie. 'I didn't hear him and I didn't see him.'

'I don't know what he looks like now,' said Edward. 'Do you?'

'No, come to think of it, I don't,' Annie admitted. 'I'm sure he wouldn't have left without saying goodbye, but where can he be?'

9

To Rescue a Prince

The house was very quiet. Edward peeped into his parents' bedroom and saw his mum and dad sitting on the bed. They were holding each other tight.

'Mum, Dad! Don't worry,' said Edward.

'It's all over. They've gone.'

'We saw them,' croaked Mrs Pugh. 'Hundreds and hundreds of dogs. What were they doing in our house?'

'It's a long story,' said Edward.

'And you probably wouldn't believe us,' added Annie.

'It was all Delilah's fault,' went on Edward. 'She put a spell on the dogs because they chased her.'

'Really, Edward!' snorted Mrs Pugh, almost herself again. 'What will you think of next?'

'It's true, Mum,' said Edward. 'But Delilah's promised never to make spells again or,' he put his mouth close to the box, 'I'll give her a bath!'

Inside the box Delilah said something very rude but luckily no one could understand her. It just sounded like a long snarl that ended in a spit.

'I think she's got the message,' said Annie. 'Come on, we've got to find Prince.'

She ran downstairs and out into the garden, calling, 'Prince! Prince, where are you?'

From somewhere above Annie there came a deep grating noise. She looked up. There, at the top of the tall spindly tree, perched

dangerously on a narrow branch, was a huge St Bernard.

'Prince?' Annie inquired, in disbelief.

The great dog barked something that sounded like 'Yes'.

'I wish you could still talk,' said Annie.

Prince barked again.

'Are you stuck?'

This time the big dog howled like a ship in distress and the few leaves that remained on the tree were torn away and blown into the sky like a cloud of sparrows.

'Whatever was that?' asked Mr Watkin, who happened to be cleaning his trainers on the back step. Then he saw Prince. 'Good grief!' he exclaimed, jumping up. 'How did a St Bernard get up there? And what are you doing in next-door's garden, Annie?'

'It would take too long to explain,' said Annie. 'But please, ring the fire brigade or someone, quickly, Dad. I think Prince is going to fall and he belongs to Dora Bell.'

'Dora Bell?' Mr Watkin laced up his trainers and leapt over the garden wall.

By this time the Pughs had run into their garden and Mrs Watkin had come out to see why there was a foghorn so close by. They all stared up at the St Bernard in amazement.

'I'll ring the fire brigade,' said Mrs Watkin.

'Wait!' commanded her husband. 'I'm going to rescue that dog myself. What's the use of being two metres and two centimetres tall if you can't rescue a Prince from a tree?'

'Rather risky!' remarked Mr Pugh, who wasn't much above one metre and a half. 'But you can borrow my ladder if you like.'

'That's very neighbourly,' said Mr Watkin warmly.

'Well, it is our tree,' Mr Pugh pointed out.

'I'm still ringing the fire brigade,' declared sensible Mrs Watkin.

'You'd better ring Dora Bell as well,' said Annie. 'It's her dog.'

Mr Pugh brought his ladder out of the garage and set it against the spindly tree.

Mr Watkin rolled up his sleeves and

mounted the ladder. Unfortunately, the ladder didn't reach the branch where Prince was sitting so Mr Watkin had to do some awkward climbing. When he was on the branch immediately beneath Prince he began to talk to the dog, very softly. He even tried some gentle humming. Prince answered with

long deep barks which set the tree swaying rather dangerously. Then, very slowly, the big dog lowered himself on to Mr Watkin's back. Mr Watkin groaned as he took Prince's weight but he clung on bravely.

'The fire brigade will be here soon,' cried Mrs Watkin hurrying up to the wall.

'Your husband is a hero, Mrs Watkin,' exclaimed Mrs Pugh.

'Please call me Pam,' said Mrs Watkin.

'My name's Grizelda,' Mrs Pugh confided shyly.

'STOP TALKING!' shouted Edward. 'Any sound may be the last straw.'

Annie was pleased to see him taking such a firm stand with his mother.

Edward put Delilah's box on the ground and sat on it while everyone stopped talking and watched Mr Watkin climb very, very carefully down the tree. Prince clung to his back as still and silent as a stone. Mr Watkin reached the ladder. He put one foot on the top rung and – SNAP – it broke in two.

'Oooooooo!' everyone moaned.

And Mrs Pugh cried, 'Oh dear! I knew the ladder wasn't strong enough. That dog must weigh a ton. Can they hang on until the fire brigade gets here?'

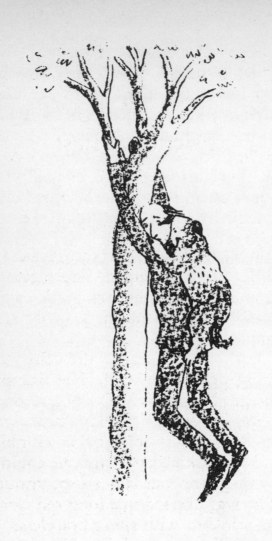

10

Friends at Last

No one dared speak. They all held their breath for what seemed like ages. They waited and watched the tree until Annie was sure that Prince and her dad would crash to the ground.

At last, they heard the fire engine screeching down the road. The firemen ran into the garden and when they had put their long steel ladder over Mr Pugh's rickety ladder, one of the firemen began climbing up to help Mr Watkin. But before he could reach him a very glamorous lady swept through the gate. She was dressed in a long red cloak and her arms tinkled with silver bracelets.

'Dora Bell,' breathed Mr Watkin, nearly forgetting where he was.

'What a hero!' cried Dora Bell. 'You've saved my Prince.'

'That's my dad,' said Annie, pointing proudly at Mr Watkin.

They all watched while Mr Watkin slowly descended the firemen's ladder. He was panting very hard and the fireman behind him had to support Prince's rather large bottom. But at last they were on the ground. Dora Bell hugged and kissed Prince, and then she hugged and kissed Mr Watkin who went as red as the lipstick she left on his cheek.

'Tea, everyone?' called Mrs Watkin, who had appeared with a tray of tea and cakes.

'Pam, you're a marvel,' said Mrs Pugh.

But before anyone could take a cup there was a shriek and a flash, a hiss and a spit and Delilah burst out of the box.

'Whatever's that?' cried Dora Bell.

'That's Delilah,' Edward told her. 'She caused all the trouble. But she's never going to do it again, are you Delilah?' he said forcefully.

Delilah bared her gleaming teeth. She flexed her shiny claws and scowled at Edward as if to say, 'How dare you talk to me like that!' Then she turned her back on them all and walked away, her big smoky tail held very high.

'What an extraordinary, amazing and

unbelievable creature,' remarked Dora Bell.
'She makes me feel all shivery. Why I could
almost believe she was – a witch.'

'She is!' said Annie and Edward.

Everyone else smiled and started talking to
each other and eating cake, but Annie noticed
that Prince was gazing after Delilah with a
rather eager expression.

'Prince!' whispered Annie. 'You must
promise never to chase Delilah again, or any
other cat for that matter.'

Prince looked at Annie and gave a long
forlorn bark. It sounded like a promise. But
Delilah stopped in her tracks and crouched on
the ground. She looked angry and, somehow,

very lonely. Suddenly, Annie found herself
walking quietly to the fierce forbidding cat
and stroking her very gently between the
ears.

'It's all right, Delilah,' she said softly.

'You're quite safe now. Aren't you lovely?'

And, as if in answer, there came from Delilah a tiny sound, like a faraway drum, that grew and grew into a deep contented purr.

'There,' said Annie. 'I knew you could.'

'I don't believe it!' said Edward. 'I thought she'd never purr.' He came and stroked Delilah's back.

Prince watched them for a moment and then he padded over to them and sat quite still, listening to the friendly purring of the strange grey cat and, in his own way, smiling.

Later, when all the firemen and all the cakes had disappeared, the Pughs and the Watkins shook hands with Prince and Dora Bell and saw them to their car.

Just before she stepped inside, Dora Bell said, 'I wish Prince could tell me how all this happened.'

Prince looked at Annie over his shoulder and Annie said, 'I expect he was bewitched!'

Dora Bell laughed. 'I suppose you're going to tell me it was that cat,' she cried.

Annie and Edward looked at each other but this time they didn't say a word.

11

A Queen at Home

It is after midnight. Delilah is sitting on the wall, a queen of the night-garden. She is safe and happy. The dogs in this neighbourhood respect her; word has got about that she is a cat of distinction and mysterious power. Mind you, Delilah has been far too busy lately to think of spells. Annie-next-door has a new pet, a pushy little kitten called Tudor; he is black and very mischievous. Delilah has had her work cut out licking him into shape. But it is work she enjoys.

She is glad she came to this house. Everyone is happy. Everyone is friendly. Sometimes she thinks of her mother and, sometimes, she thinks of Mustapha Marzavan and his great cat-parlour, but she feels at home here now. Every morning Annie-next-door comes to see her, and when Delilah closes her eyes she can recognise the soft voice and gentle hand of Mustapha Marzavan's youngest daughter.

And Delilah purrs.